Dink, Josh, and Ruth Rose aren't the only kid detectives!

What about you?

Can you find the hidden message inside this book?

There are 26 illustrations in this book, not counting the one on the title page, the map at the beginning, and the picture of the queen's jewels that repeats at the start of many of the chapters. In each of the 26 illustrations, there's a hidden letter. If you can find all the letters, you will spell out a secret message!

If you're stumped, the answer is on the bottom of page 135.

Happy detecting!

This book is dedicated to travelers,
dreamers, and readers.
—R.R.

To George Alexander Louis,
Prince of Cambridge
—J.S.G.

Text copyright © 2014 by Ron Roy
Cover art and interior illustrations copyright © 2014 by John Steven Gurney

Visit us on the Web!
SteppingStonesBooks.com
randomhouse.com/kids

Educators and librarians, for a variety of teaching tools,
visit us at RHTeachersLibrarians.com

Library of Congress Cataloging-in-Publication Data
Roy, Ron.
The castle crime / by Ron Roy ; illustrated by John Steven Gurney.
pages cm. — (A to Z mysteries. Super edition ; #6)
"A Stepping Stone book."
Summary: While visiting London, Dink, Josh, and Ruth Rose solve a mystery and meet the Queen.
ISBN 978-0-385-37159-9 (trade) — ISBN 978-0-385-37160-5 (lib. bdg.) — ISBN 978-0-385-37161-2 (ebook)
[1. Mystery and detective stories. 2. Robbers and outlaws—Fiction. 3. London (England)—Fiction. 4. England—Fiction.] I. Gurney, John Steven, illustrator. II. Title.
PZ7.R8139Cas 2014 [Fic]—dc23 2013005012

Printed in the United States of America
10 9 8 7 6 5 4 3 2 1

A to Z Mysteries®

Super Edition #6

The Castle Crime

by Ron Roy

illustrated by
John Steven Gurney

A STEPPING STONE BOOK™

Random House   New York

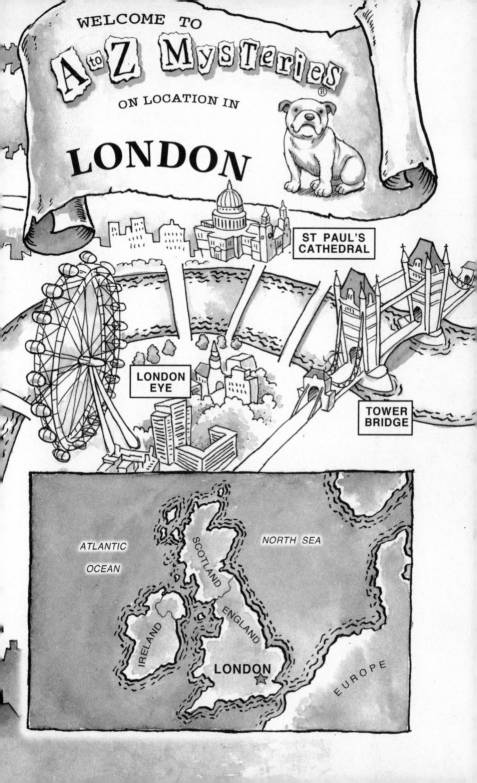

CHAPTER 1

"Watch the traffic," Dink's father warned Dink, Josh, and Ruth Rose. "Don't forget, they drive on the left here in England."

They all stood across the road from the Madame Tussauds wax museum in London, England. The building was long, gray, and wet.

Dink's father was in London for a conference and had invited the three kids along. It was their first trip to Europe. So far, they'd visited the Big Ben clock, Buckingham Palace, and the Tower of London.

Last night, the four had gone on a Jack the Ripper walking tour. A guide showed them the streets and alleys where a murderer killed several women in 1888. The murderer was never caught.

Yesterday they had ridden on a huge Ferris wheel called the London Eye. From the top, almost 450 feet off the ground, the kids could see most of London. When a helicopter zoomed past them, the pilot and Josh waved at each other.

"Let's cross," Mr. Duncan said, stepping over a puddle. It was raining lightly. Cars and buses swished past them, splashing water onto the sidewalks.

"Ian, our tour guide, will meet us at entrance number one," Dink's father said.

He and the kids stood in front of the

museum. A sign on the building said MADAME TUSSAUDS. They saw an orange door with a big numeral 1 over it.

"Let me get a picture," Ruth Rose said. She pulled a small purple camera from her purple backpack. Her jeans, jacket, boots, and headband were also purple. Ruth Rose's outfits always matched. They were a different color each day.

"Cool!" Josh said. He ran his fingers through his damp red hair.

"Smile!" Ruth Rose said, aiming her camera. Standing in front of Mr. Duncan, Dink and Josh slung their arms around each other's shoulders. Dink grinned at the camera, but Josh made a goofy face.

"How do I look?" Josh asked, crossing his eyes.

"Like you've lost your mind," Ruth Rose said. She pushed the button and got the shot.

"What mind?" Dink asked, giving Josh a shove.

The three kids were best friends. They lived in Green Lawn, Connecticut, more than three thousand miles away from London.

"Let's go inside," Dink's father said. "It's starting to rain harder." They walked toward the door.

"So who's Madame Tussaud?" Josh asked.

"Her married name was Tussaud, but she was born Anna Maria Grosholtz," Ruth Rose said. "She was born in France in 1761. She learned how to make wax figures that looked like real people and opened a museum here in London. People paid money to see the figures."

"How do you know all this stuff?" Josh asked Ruth Rose.

She showed him her London guidebook. "I studied on the plane," she said.

"You kids ready?" Dink's father asked as he rang the bell next to the orange door.

The door opened and a tall, thin man peered out at them. He wore black-rimmed eyeglasses. A name tag on his shirt said IAN. "Hi! Are you the Duncans from the States?" he asked.

Ian had spiky black hair. The tips of the spikes were bleached yellow.

"I'm Mr. Duncan," Dink's father told Ian. "This is my son, Dink, and his friends Josh and Ruth Rose."

"Great, come on in," Ian said. He glanced at his watch.

"Sorry to get here so late," Mr. Duncan said. "I was at a conference and just got out a few minutes ago."

"No problem," Ian said. "We still have twenty minutes before we close. And you can always come back tomorrow if you want."

They followed Ian into a lobby with a ticket counter. The walls were covered with posters of famous people. A giant chandelier hung from the tall ceiling. Dink noticed a stack of bumper stickers for sale. They had MADAME TUSSAUDS printed in bold black letters. *Maybe I'll buy one on the way out,* he thought.

A tall woman walked up to the group. Her name tag said MANDY. She was dressed in a yellow sweatshirt with a picture of Madame Tussauds on the front. She wore bright pink lipstick and green eye shadow. She was chewing gum and holding a cell phone.

"For you," Mandy said, handing the phone to Ian.

Ian took the phone. "Will you excuse me?" he said to Dink's father and the kids. "Mandy, would you take over?"

"Sure," Mandy said as Ian walked away.

"Are you a guide, too?" Ruth Rose asked.

"No, but I fill in sometimes. I usually work on the wax heads, making sure the faces look real," Mandy said. "I love using makeup!"

A small TV was perched on a shelf behind the ticket counter. The news was on, and a man with wavy hair was talking with a British accent.

"He doesn't sound like you," Josh said to Mandy. "Are you from here?"

Mandy shook her head. "No, I'm from California."

"Cool!" Dink said. "Have you ever seen any movie stars?"

"Plenty," Mandy said. "I worked in special effects at one of the movie studios. We turned actors into monsters with wigs, makeup, masks, fake claws, and lots of fake blood!"

"That is awesome!" Josh said.

"So, have you kids ever been to a

Madame Tussauds wax museum before?" Mandy asked.

Mr. Duncan and the kids shook their heads.

"Is there more than one?" Dink asked.

"Yes," Mandy said. "There are sixteen now. You have four in the United States: in New York, Las Vegas, Washington, D.C., and Los Angeles. There are other branches all over the world."

Josh was staring at the TV set. "Guys, did you hear that?" he asked. "He just said the Queen of England got robbed!"

Mandy walked over and turned down the sound. "It happened yesterday, on her birthday," she said.

"The Queen of England was born on April twenty-first?" Ruth Rose asked.

Mandy nodded. "In 1926, I think."

"So what happened?" Dink asked.

"The queen was driving to Windsor Castle yesterday for her birthday party," Mandy said. "She brought some of her favorite jewels with her. When she stopped the car, one of the robbers reached through the window and grabbed her jewel case."

"Why did she stop?" Ruth Rose asked.

"The robbers were disguised as her grandsons Prince William and Prince Harry," Mandy explained. "They were wearing lifelike rubber masks. William and Harry are both in the military, so the robbers wore uniforms like theirs. I guess the queen thought the robbers were her grandsons, so she stopped and rolled down the window."

"Wow!" Josh said. "So did they catch the guys? Did they find the jewels?"

"No," Mandy said.

"Where's Windsor Castle?" Ruth Rose asked. "I read that the queen lives here in London at Buckingham Palace."

"Yes, you're right," Mandy said. "But Windsor Castle is only a short drive away, and the queen likes to go there some weekends. Her husband and Prince Charles were there, planning her party. The two grandsons secretly showed up to surprise her."

"Wait, I'm confused," Dink said. "You said the robbers were dressed up to look like her grandsons. Where were the real grandsons?"

"The real Princes William and Harry were inside Windsor Castle waiting for her to arrive," Mandy explained. "But the queen didn't know that, of course. So when she saw the two robbers outside the castle grounds, she thought *they* were her grandsons. When she stopped, they snatched her jewels."

"But how did the robbers know the queen would be driving to Windsor Castle that day?" Josh asked.

"And how did they know she'd have those jewels with her?" Ruth Rose added.

Mandy shrugged. "I guess we'll never know," she said.

"What did the queen do after she got robbed?" Ruth Rose asked. Dink noticed that Ruth Rose's eyes were opened wide.

"She drove to the castle and called the police at Scotland Yard," Mandy said.

CHAPTER 2

Mandy led the kids through a pair of black curtains. On the other side, they saw a roomful of people. Only they weren't real people. They were man-made statues that *looked* alive. A few tourists were wandering around.

"Oh my gosh!" Josh said. "There's Johnny Depp!"

"And Kate Winslet!" exclaimed Ruth Rose.

"And John Wayne!" Dink added.

"They look so real!" Josh said. "Are they all made of wax?" he asked Mandy.

"The heads are sculpted from wax, but not the bodies," Mandy said. She tapped on Babe Ruth's arm. It sounded hard, like plastic.

"Long ago, Madame Tussaud used wax for the bodies as well," Mandy explained. "But wax melts and shrinks, so now we make the bodies out of fiberglass."

"Mandy, how long does it take to make one of these?" Dink's father asked.

"About four months," Mandy said. "If you come back another day, you can meet some of the artists who create them."

Ruth Rose walked up close to the figure of a beautiful blond woman. "Is this Marilyn Monroe?" she whispered.

Mandy smiled. "Gorgeous, isn't she?"

The famous movie star was wearing diamonds. "Are her diamonds real?" Dink asked.

"Nope. They're fake, just like all the jewelry in the museum," Mandy said.

"How about their hair?" Josh asked. He was standing next to a statue with long hair and a flowing beard.

"It's all real human hair," Mandy told them. "And each hair was placed in the wax head by hand, with tweezers, one hair at a time."

"Wow!" Dink said. "That must take forever!"

Mandy smiled. "About six weeks to do a head of hair," she said, pointing to Elvis Presley. "We put about ten thousand hairs in Elvis's head."

"What do you do when the hair gets dirty?" Ruth Rose asked.

"We shampoo it," Mandy said. "That's why we use real human hair. We can even style it and cut it, the way you do with your own hair."

They walked through another pair

of black curtains. Suddenly they were in a room with red velvet walls, fancy furniture, and soft lighting from electric candles.

"This is the world leaders' room," Mandy told the kids.

Ian was talking to a small group of tourists. He was explaining how the wax heads were made.

Dink walked over to the figure of a woman with reddish hair. She was dressed in a black suit. He read a sign that said she was Margaret Thatcher. She had been the prime minister of the United Kingdom.

Ruth Rose and Josh were reading the sign, too. "So she was like the president of England," Ruth Rose said. "Cool. She was the big boss!"

"Look, there's our president!" Josh said. He walked over to the current president. He wore a dark blue suit and red tie. He was smiling and looked very real.

"Where do you get the clothes?" Ruth Rose asked.

"Usually, the subject gives us two sets of clothing," Mandy said. "We dress the statue in one set, and the other is kept in our wardrobe room for emergencies."

"What kind of emergency?" Josh asked.

"Well, as you can see, people like to walk right up and touch the statues," Mandy said. "So the clothing gets dirty, smelly, even ripped sometimes. Once, a little boy threw up on David Beckham's uniform!"

"Gross!" Josh blurted out.

Mandy smiled. "Totally," she said. "So we just changed Beckham into his spare uniform."

"There's so much to see!" Dink said.

There were more than forty world leaders in this room.

"You'll have more time on your next visit," Mandy said. She looked at her watch. "We close in ten minutes, but your London Pass lets you come back as often as you want."

"Is the Queen of England's figure here?" Ruth Rose asked.

"She's in the next room," Mandy said. "Follow me."

On the other side of some black curtains was Queen Elizabeth. She stood next to a red-and-gold chair. Gathered around the queen were her husband, Prince Philip; their son Prince Charles; and the queen's grandsons Prince William and Prince Harry.

Metal poles held a red velvet rope that stretched around the Royal Family, keeping the kids and Mr. Duncan about ten feet away.

"Why is this rope here, but not around any of the other figures?" Josh asked.

Mandy rested her hand on the rope. "To keep people away from the queen," she said. "Too many tourists like touching her."

"Wow," Dink said. "They all look so real!"

"Yes," Mandy said. "William and Harry came in not long ago to have their pictures taken with their wax figures. We could hardly tell them apart!"

"The men are a lot taller than the queen," Dink said.

"She's average height," Mandy said. "About five feet, five inches. Her son Charles is nearly six feet, and both grandsons are about six-three."

"Even the fake diamonds look real," Ruth Rose said.

The queen wore a diamond tiara on

her white hair, and a fabulous diamond necklace around her neck.

"Yes, these were made to look identical to the queen's own jewels," Mandy said. "In fact, it was her tiara and necklace that were stolen yesterday."

The four stared at the Royal Family. Prince William had blond hair and wore a navy-blue jacket and a black tie. His cap was black and had a wide red band over the bill.

His brother, Harry, had orangey-red hair. He was wearing a red tunic with silver buttons. A white belt was cinched around his waist. The silver belt buckle gleamed under the lights. Both men wore white trousers, white cotton gloves, and black shoes.

"It almost seems like they could wake up and walk around," Dink said.

"How do they make the eyes look so real?" Josh asked.

Mandy tapped her watch. "I can show you, but not today," she said.

As they passed through the black curtains, Dink noticed a man standing near Albert Einstein. He was holding a sketch pad and a pencil.

"I should have brought my sketching stuff," Josh said.

The kids watched the man making swift marks on his pad. He was tall and had a short beard. His hair was hidden under a baseball cap.

Mandy walked up to the man. "Sorry, sir, but we're closing in a few minutes."

The man nodded, closed his pad, and strolled toward the exit.

As Mandy led the group out, Ruth Rose peeked into an open doorway. "Oh, is this where the extra clothes are kept?" she asked.

"Yes," Mandy said. "Want a quick peek?"

She led them into a large room with a carpet on the floor. Everywhere the kids looked were racks of clothing. Each rack was inside a glass case. Dink noticed a small, round lock on each case. Above the glass cases were shelves holding fake jewelry, wigs, hats, beards, even a row of false teeth.

A short woman with gray hair sat at a table in a corner. She was stitching a pink dress. Three fingers on each hand were wrapped in Band-Aids. On the table were scissors, a jar of pins, and a tape measure. A ring of keys lay next to the scissors.

"Sofia is repairing a gown that ripped when someone stepped on it," Mandy said.

"Why does she have all those Band-Aids on?" Ruth Rose asked.

"To protect her fingers," Mandy said. "Those scissors and needles are sharp!"

Sofia looked up, smiled at the kids, and went back to her work.

In another corner, Dink noticed a small desk with a bulletin board above it. A few pictures had been pinned to the cork. Dink recognized Mandy with a smiling man in one picture. In another, Mandy was hugging a dog, with ocean water in the background.

Next to the desk were a sink and mirror under a small window. A row of miniature bottles sat on a shelf above the window. Each bottle was filled with a different-colored liquid.

"What's in those little jars?" Dink asked.

"Paint," Mandy said. "We use it for quick repairs. The shoes get scuffed up a lot from tourists stepping on them. Sometimes our cleaning crew's vacuum cleaners bang up against the shoes. When that happens, we just choose the right paint color and touch up the scuff. If it gets real bad, we replace the shoe."

Josh pointed to a jar of glass eyes. "They look like marbles!" he said. "Marbles that stare at you!"

"Those are old," Mandy said. "We have better methods for making eyes now. If you come back, I'll show you how we do it."

She waved a hand around the room.

"As you can see, we have thousands of clothing changes," she went on. "If that little boy vomits on anyone else, we can get that outfit dry-cleaned and dress the figure in the spare outfit."

"This is amazing," Josh said. They were surrounded by hundreds of suits, jackets, dresses, fur coats, hats, scarves, canes, and uniforms. One rack held hundreds of neckties.

"Why is everything inside those cases?" Dink asked.

"To protect the clothing from getting dusty," Mandy said.

"How do you find what you need?" Ruth Rose asked.

"Each rack is labeled," Mandy said. "For example, world leaders, the Royal Family, and sports figures are all on separate racks. And each outfit has a tag with the figure's name. Of course, every item of clothing is also in our computer."

They heard a soft bell sound.

"Six o'clock, closing time," Mandy said. She led the kids and Dink's dad toward the exit.

CHAPTER 3

It was still raining when they left the museum.

"I have to check in at the conference one last time," Dink's father said. "I'll meet you at the hotel later."

"Okay, bye, Dad," Dink said. Josh and Ruth Rose waved.

Mr. Duncan stepped to the curb and raised his hand for a taxi. A shiny black cab pulled over, and Mr. Duncan stepped inside. He waved as the cab sped away.

"Race you back!" Ruth Rose yelled. Hopping over puddles, they dashed to their hotel, around the corner from the museum. Soon they burst into the hotel lobby, damp and laughing.

The hotel was called Welcome House. Two hundred years earlier, the small brick building had been a private home. Dink's father had picked it because it was close to the museum, shops, and restaurants.

A small plaque near the doorbell read:

IN 1888, JACK THE RIPPER MURDERED AT LEAST FIVE WOMEN IN LONDON. ONE OF THE VICTIMS LIVED IN THIS BUILDING. THE UNKNOWN KILLER WAS NEVER CAUGHT.

"They never caught the guy," Josh whispered. He poked Dink's back.

Dink shivered. "When we were on the tour last night, I kept thinking Jack the Ripper was following us," he said. "Those dark, narrow streets were creepy!"

"He must be dead, Dink," Ruth Rose said. She rang the bell. "If Jack the Ripper was alive, he'd be at least 150 years old!"

"But what if his *ghost* was following us?" Josh whispered. "What if his next victim is a kid named Dink? What if—"

A tall man with red hair opened the door. The name tag pinned to his sweater said DAMON FOX, MANAGER.

"How was the museum?" Damon asked. "I assume Ian took good care of you."

The kids followed Damon into the lobby.

"You know Ian?" Dink asked.

"He's my cousin," Damon said.

"We saw all these amazing fake people," Josh said. "Hey, has anyone ever told you that you look like Prince Harry?"

Damon Fox blushed. "Yes, I've heard

that quite a few times," he said.

"Did you hear about the queen's jewels getting stolen?" Ruth Rose asked Damon.

He nodded. "It's been on TV for two days, and the story's in all the news-papers," he said.

He reached toward a stack of *London Times* papers at one end of the counter.

"Take one with you if you'd like," he said, handing Dink a paper. Dink noticed a round bandage stuck to the back of Damon's left hand.

Welcome House had no elevator, so the kids climbed the stairs to their rooms on the second floor. Dink shared a room with Josh, and Ruth Rose had the one next door. Dink's father's room was across the hall.

In Dink and Josh's room, the three kids grabbed bed pillows and flopped on the floor. Josh turned on the TV set and Dink opened the newspaper.

A weather forecast was on TV. The weatherwoman was apologizing for all the rain. "Rain yesterday, rain today, more rain tonight," she said. "Typical April weather in England!"

"Hey, look, here's a story about the queen's jewelry!" Dink said.

He read the headline:

THE  TIMES

A Royal Mystery!

No news yet on the whereabouts of the queen's filched jewels. The two men who snatched the jewels yesterday, on the queen's birthday, are still at large.

But the queen did give the detectives from Scotland Yard information that may be helpful. It seems that her dog bit the hand that reached through her window for the jewel case.

The queen also reported that a black car was parked on the road a few meters from the castle's main gate, where the robbery took place. She watched the two robbers—disguised as her grandsons—leap into the car and speed off in the rain. In her rearview mirror, the queen noticed a white bumper sticker on their car. She told Scotland Yard that mud covered part of the bumper sticker. But she remembers seeing the letters *U-A-S-S* and *E-M-A-D*.

Any citizen who has information may contact Inspector Grabbe at Scotland Yard.

The Royal Family is offering a reward of ten thousand pounds for information leading to the arrest of the thieves or the recovery of the stolen jewels.

Below the story was a picture of the queen wearing a tiara and necklace like the ones the kids had seen on her wax figure.

"There's a reward?" Josh said. "Cool, we should try to get it! How much is ten thousand pounds in American money?"

"Wait a second," Ruth Rose said. She pulled her guidebook out of her backpack. She flipped a few pages. "Here it is." She counted silently for a few seconds. "Ten thousand British pounds is around fifteen thousand U.S. dollars."

"Oh my gosh!" Josh said. He did a little math on his fingers. "That means if we solve the crime, we each get about five thousand dollars!"

"Dude, don't start spending that money," Dink said. He flipped his pillow at Josh. "If Scotland Yard can't find these guys, three fourth graders sure can't."

Josh tapped his head. "But they don't have the mighty Josh brain!" he said.

Dink fell over laughing. "You don't, either!" he said.

Ruth Rose clicked off the TV set. She stared at Dink and Josh. "What if we *could* solve *the Royal Mystery*?" she asked quietly.

Josh looked at her. "Are you serious?"

Ruth Rose nodded. "Why not? We have a couple more days before we go home."

"But how?" Dink asked. "We don't know anything."

"Sure we do." Ruth Rose held up five fingers. "One: the queen left Buckingham Palace with her jewels. Two: she drove to Windsor Castle. Three: she saw her two grandsons standing in the rain."

"Except they weren't really her grandsons," Josh put in.

"I know," Ruth Rose said. "Then, four: she stopped and rolled down her window. Five: one of the robbers reached in and grabbed the jewel case."

"And number six, her pooch bit the guy," Josh said.

"And seven, the queen saw some letters on a bumper sticker," Dink added.

Ruth Rose found that part of the newspaper story. "*U-A-S-S* and *E-M-A-D*," she read out loud. "Eight letters. Are they words?"

"Yeah," Josh joked, "in some other language."

"I wonder what they mean," Dink said.

Josh stretched out on the floor and looked at the ceiling. "It means Josh solves the mystery!" he said. "I want a helicopter like the one we saw the other day! Do you think I can buy a helicopter with fifteen thousand dollars?"

Dink and Ruth Rose laughed.

Then they heard something outside the bedroom door.

Whatever it was made a soft scratching noise.

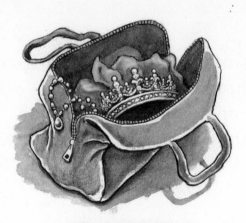

CHAPTER 4

Dink walked to the door. He listened but didn't hear anything else. "Who is it?" he asked.

"Jack," a deep voice said. Dink heard more scratching. "Let me in."

Dink gulped. "Jack who?" he asked.

Then he heard his father's laugh. "Jack the Ripper!"

Dink unlocked the door and yanked it open. "Very funny, Dad," Dink said.

"*I* thought so," Mr. Duncan said. He walked into the room and took off his damp jacket and cap.

"Mr. Duncan, we've been reading more about the queen's jewels being stolen," Josh said.

Dink's dad nodded. "It's all anyone's talking about," he said. "Unbelievable how the robbers pulled it off. Imagine disguising themselves as the queen's own grandsons!"

"It could have been an inside job!" Josh said. "I'll bet someone at Buckingham Palace stole the jewels!"

"Yeah," Dink said. "Maybe the butler did it!"

Mr. Duncan smiled. "Sounds like you kids want to solve another mystery," he said.

"There's a monster reward!" Josh said.

Mr. Duncan walked back to the door. "I'm taking us out to dinner tonight," he said, looking at his watch. "How about seven-thirty?"

"Thanks, Dad," Dink said. "See you later."

"Keep your door locked," Mr. Duncan said to Dink. "They never caught Jack the Ripper. He might be hiding around here somewhere!"

Dink laughed. "Josh will protect us," he said. But he locked the door behind his father.

"I still think the robbers might be someone in Buckingham Palace," Josh said.

"You mean someone who works there?" Dink asked. He flopped on his bed.

"Yeah," Josh said. "In the movies, it's always the butler or the gardener."

"Well, if it was an inside job," Ruth Rose said, "why wouldn't it be someone at Windsor Castle? She was driving there for her birthday party."

"You're right," Dink said. "The newspaper said she stopped her car a few meters from the Windsor Castle gate."

"How much is a meter?" Josh asked.

Ruth Rose grabbed her guidebook and flipped to the index. "A meter is a little more than one yard," she said.

"And she saw the getaway car!" Josh added. "Maybe she remembers the license plate number."

"She told the police about the bumper sticker," Dink said. "But no license plate."

Ruth Rose sat on the end of Dink's bed.

Josh stretched out on his own bed.

They looked at each other.

"We should go to Windsor Castle," Ruth Rose announced.

"Why?" Dink asked.

"To look for clues," Ruth Rose said.

Josh sat up. "What kind of clues?" he asked.

"We won't know until we find them, Josh!" Ruth Rose said.

Josh grinned at her and Dink. "So when do you want to go?"

"Really?" Ruth Rose said.

"Sure, why not?" Josh said. "It would be cool to have our pictures in the *London Times.* 'Connecticut Kids Catch Crooks.' "

"We can go tomorrow," Ruth Rose said. "I'll ask Damon how to get there."

The next morning, the kids crowded in front of Damon at the hotel counter. "We want to go to Windsor Castle," Ruth Rose said. "How do we get there?" Today her color was blue, from her sneakers to her hat.

"Easy peasy," Damon said. "Walk along Baker Street until you get to Marylebone Road, then go stand on the other side of Marylebone. Watch for bus twenty-three. There will be a lot of other buses, so be sure to wait for the one that says *Berkshire* or *Windsor Castle*."

"What's *Berkshire*?" Dink asked.

"The county where Windsor Castle is located," Damon said.

"Can we use our London Passes?" Dink asked.

Damon nodded. "Yes, but only so many people are allowed into the castle at one time. You may not be able to get on a tour today. The grounds are beautiful, though, and you can walk around. You might even see deer or peacocks!"

"Thanks, Damon," Ruth Rose said.

"Have fun," he said. "And watch those peacocks. They like to bite tourists!"

The kids hurried up Baker Street. They crossed Marylebone Road and stood next to a bus stop sign.

"It *would* have to rain again," Josh

said. He was wearing a hooded sweatshirt. Dink and Ruth Rose wore baseball
caps.

"But it's only light rain," Dink com-
mented. "Back home, it *pours* in April."

They watched several buses go by.
None was number 23.

Cars and trucks whizzed by, splatter-
ing rain everywhere.

Finally, the right bus came along.
They showed the driver their London
Passes.

"We're going to see Windsor Castle,"
Dink said.

The driver grinned. "Be careful not
to get close to the peacocks," he said.
"They'll take one of your fingers clean
off you!"

The kids sat behind the driver.
Twenty-five minutes later, he pulled up
to a tall fence. The gate was open.

"Just walk up that long drive to the

castle," the driver said. "A bus comes here about every forty-five minutes, till six. After that, you're on your own."

The kids hopped off the bus and walked through the black iron gates. Soft rain plopped on the trees, bushes, and bright green lawn.

The first thing they saw was a peacock with his tail in the air. He stared at the kids with shiny black eyes.

The kids stopped.

"He doesn't look happy to see us," Josh whispered.

"Why don't you go pet him?" Dink asked.

"No way!" Josh said. "I like having ten fingers!"

Ruth Rose opened her pack. She pulled out a small bunch of grapes that she'd snitched from breakfast. "Watch this," she said.

Ruth Rose waved the grapes toward

the peacock. Then she threw them as far as she could. When the peacock chased the fruit, the kids ran up the long drive.

"Nice arm," Josh told Ruth Rose.

"Easy peasy," Ruth Rose said.

CHAPTER 5

Up ahead of them, tall bushes lined the narrow drive. To Dink, it was like walking through a wet green tunnel. On both sides, the bushes dripped water.

Josh stopped walking. He pointed between two bushes. "I think I just saw a troll," he whispered.

"Trolls live under bridges," Ruth Rose said.

"No, really," Josh said.

He pointed between some bushes on their left side. "I know I saw something moving back there. It was pushing

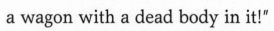

a wagon with a dead body in it!"

The three kids stopped walking and tried to peer through the bushes. They heard swishing noises.

Dink saw something dark moving. It was hunched over, and it *did* look like a troll!

"It's probably just a peacock," Ruth Rose said.

"Maybe it's a deer," Dink said. He hoped he was right.

Then they heard a clunk and something thudding on the ground.

"That's a noisy deer," Josh whispered.

They saw a shadowy figure, who suddenly stepped out from behind the bushes. He was hunched over a wheelbarrow, pushing it across the drive. The man was tall. He wore jeans, a rain hat and jacket, and rubber boots. The wheelbarrow held plants, gardening tools, and a long shovel.

"Just a gardener," Ruth Rose said. "Not a troll. And no dead body!"

"I'll bet he's one of the robbers," Josh whispered. "He's probably hiding the queen's jewels under all that stuff in the wheelbarrow."

"Gee, Josh, why don't you tackle him, then call those detectives at Scotland Yard?" Ruth Rose asked. "You'll get the reward!"

"I *know* he's a robber," Josh said under his breath. "I can tell by the way he's staring at us."

Dink grinned. "He's staring at *you!*" he said. "He's never seen so many freckles before!"

When the kids got closer, they discovered that the wheelbarrow pusher was a woman. She smiled at the kids.

"Nice weather, eh?" the woman said. Her cheeks and the tip of her nose were red. Frizzy brown hair surrounded her

face. Rain dripped off her hat.

"Does it always rain in England?" Josh asked.

The woman nodded. "Especially in April," she said. "If you're here for a castle tour, the next one isn't until two o'clock. But you can hike around, if you like getting wet!"

Ruth Rose pulled a small umbrella out of her pack. "My guidebook says always bring one with you to England!" she said.

The woman grinned at the kids. "Mind the peacocks. They like to bite kids from the United States."

"How can you tell that's where we're from?" Josh asked.

The woman laughed. "You've got funny accents, luv," she said.

Dink remembered that Mandy had said Prince William and his brother were very tall. The robbers must be tall, too, he figured. Otherwise, how could the queen have been fooled?

The woman standing in front of them was at least six feet tall.

Could Josh be right? Dink wondered. Could this friendly woman be one of the robbers?

"Are there any tall guys working here?" Dink asked the woman.

She laughed. "Only me, luv. All the men are shorties!" she said, then pushed her wheelbarrow onto a field.

The kids hiked along the drive. Fields of tall grass and wildflowers grew on both sides. A few ancient trees dripped rainwater. A grazing deer noticed the kids and bounded out of sight.

In the distance, they saw the castle. It loomed out of the mist like a castle in a fairy tale. The massive stone walls gleamed in the rain.

"Gosh, that place is bigger than our

whole town back home!" Josh said.

"It's like a city," Dink said.

They heard a dog barking somewhere ahead of them. Then a voice
called, "Come, you lot!"

Three brown-and-white dogs came
running toward the kids. They were
wet and muddy. Behind them marched

a woman carrying a walking stick. She was wearing a rain hat, a matching coat, and muddy boots.

"Come away, dogs!" the woman commanded.

"Oh my gosh," whispered Ruth Rose. "It's the queen!"

As they got closer, Dink recognized

the face they had seen at the wax museum. The Queen of England had pink cheeks, white hair, and a friendly smile.

"Lovely day, isn't it?" she asked the kids.

To Dink, the queen looked like a normal person. She reminded him of the woman who worked in the post office back in Green Lawn.

"Happy birthday, Your Majesty!" Josh blurted out. "Sorry your jewels got stolen!"

The queen gave him a sharp look. Then she sighed. "Thank you, young man," she said. "I hope the Scotland Yard people do their job well." She stared off into the rain.

"Um, we saw you in the Madame Tussauds wax museum," Dink said. "You look a lot better alive. I mean, in person!"

The queen laughed. "Well, thank

you," she said. "But they did make me look younger, didn't they?"

Dink thought about the gardener they'd just spoken with. Was it possible that she *had* stolen the queen's jewels? Dink wanted to ask the queen about the tall gardener, but he didn't get a chance.

"Did the robbers really look like your grandsons?" Ruth Rose suddenly asked the queen.

"Yes, the men who robbed me were tall, like William and Harry," she said. "The uniforms they were wearing looked exactly like William and Harry's—even their caps and white gloves. But something about their faces wasn't quite right. I think it was the way they were smiling."

"We read in the paper that they were wearing rubber masks," Josh said.

"Masks?" the queen said, looking confused. "I never told the detectives at

Scotland Yard anything about masks."
She closed her eyes for a second. "But
I suppose they *could* have been wearing
masks. That would explain why their
mouths didn't seem to move. Yes, masks
would make sense."

Something the queen had just said,
or maybe something Josh said, made
Dink shut his own eyes. He was trying
to form a thought, but it disappeared as
swiftly as the wet deer they'd seen.

Suddenly the rain began to come
down harder.

Ruth Rose popped open her umbrella and held it over her head.

The dogs bolted up to the queen.
They put muddy paws all over her legs.

"Oh dear," said the queen. "You doggies are a right mess. It's back home for
us now!" She put her hand out to the
kids. "It was lovely chatting with you!"

"You too," Dink said, shaking the

queen's warm hand. "I hope you get your jewels back."

She nodded. "Yes. But for now, I'll have to get used to wearing my fake tiara and necklace. They are identical to the ones I lost. Of course, the ones on my wax figure are also fakes."

"How do you tell the real jewels from the fakes?" Ruth Rose asked. "The ones we saw on your wax figure look so real!"

"The fakes were made by a master craftsman," the queen said. "But only my own jewels have my initials engraved on the silver—a tiny *E.A.M.*, for Elizabeth Alexandra Mary."

She turned and marched toward the castle. "Home now, doggies! Mummy will give you a treat!"

The kids watched her stride toward the castle.

"That was so cool!" Josh said. "We just talked to the Queen of England!"

"We should go home, too," Ruth Rose said. "It's no fun hiking around in the rain." She checked her watch. "The next tour is in over two hours!"

They crowded under her umbrella and headed for the gate. The bus was not waiting, so they stood under a tree.

Dink looked at the road and the fence. "I wonder where the robbery took place," he said. "I mean, where did she stop her car?"

Ruth Rose walked down the wet road toward the fence. She stopped about ten feet in front of the gate. "Right about here," she said. "A few meters from the gate."

"So where was the getaway car?" Josh asked. He looked at the damp ground under their feet.

"Not too far if the queen could read letters on a bumper sticker," Dink said.

He crossed the road and walked slowly along the grass toward the fence. He was hunched over, searching with his eyes.

Ruth Rose and Josh did the same thing on the opposite side.

"Um, what're we looking for?" Josh asked.

"Tire tracks," Ruth Rose said. "If a getaway car parked here, there might be marks in the mud."

"Marks like these?" Josh asked. He pointed to four ruts in the muddy grass.

CHAPTER 6

"Exactly like those!" Ruth Rose cried.

Dink ran over, and the kids examined the marks together.

"Good eye, Josh," Dink said.

Josh tapped the side of his head and grinned. A raindrop slid off his nose. "On television, the police always pour white gooey stuff into tire marks to make molds," he said. "Then they compare the molds with the tires on the suspects' cars."

"The gooey stuff is plaster," Dink said. "And we don't have any."

He bent over and picked something shiny out of the grass.

"What is it?" Josh asked.

"Just a little diamond," Dink said.

"WHAT? YOU FOUND A DIA-MOND?" Josh yelled. He reached for Dink's hand.

Dink laughed. "Joking, Josh," he said. "It's a rolled-up piece of foil." He showed Josh and Ruth Rose a tiny silver ball.

Dink flattened the foil. When he flipped it over, they saw the words SUMMER GREEN GUM.

"It's a gum wrapper," Dink said. He held it under his nose. "It smells kind of spicy."

"It's a clue!" Ruth Rose said. "Maybe one of the robbers dropped it here!"

Josh grinned. "So now we have to find a tall guy who chews Summer Green gum," he joked. "Somewhere in England!"

Ruth Rose nodded. "And he has a tall friend," she said. "One of them drives a black car with *U-A-S-S* and *E-M-A-D* on a bumper sticker."

"And one of them might have a dog bite on his hand," Dink added.

Just then, the bus showed up. The

driver stopped in front of the kids, and the door whooshed open.

"Heck, we'll never get that reward," Josh said as the kids climbed aboard.

Forty minutes later, the kids piled into the Welcome House lobby. Damon Fox was standing behind the counter, doing paperwork.

Dink noticed a new stack of newspapers. On the front page was a large picture of the queen and her grandsons Prince William and Prince Harry.

A bold caption under the picture said:

The Royal Family is sad. Scotland Yard is still stumped over the stolen jewels.

"Hey, how was your trip?" Damon said when he saw the kids.

"We met the queen!" Josh blurted out. "She is so cool!"

"You did not!" Damon said. "You're joshing me, right?"

Dink laughed. "Josh never joshes," he said.

"The queen was walking her dogs," said Ruth Rose. "She talked with us and shook our hands!"

"Have you ever seen her?" Josh asked.

Damon ran his fingers through his red hair. "Only once," he said.

Dink dropped his eyes to the photo of Prince Harry. Then he glanced back up at Damon. The two men had the same red hair, the same pink cheeks, and the same blue eyes.

"Can we take a paper?" Dink asked, feeling himself blush at what he was thinking.

"Sure, they're here for our guests," Damon said.

Dink took a paper. "Have you seen my dad?" he asked.

Damon pointed toward the ceiling. "He's up in his room," he said. "With a large pizza!"

The kids raced up the stairs to Mr. Duncan's room. Dink knocked on the door.

"Who's there?" came his father's voice.

"Jack," Dink answered in a deep voice.

"Jack the Ripper?" asked his father. "Come in and have a slice of pizza, Jack!"

The kids walked into the room. Dink's father was sitting on the sofa with a book on his lap. A slice of pizza and a napkin sat on a small table near his elbow.

"Hey, kids, how was your morning?" Mr. Duncan asked.

They took turns telling him how they met the queen.

"No fair!" Dink's father said. "I've

been to London three times, and I've never seen her once!"

Dink showed the front page of the newspaper to his father. "They still haven't found the queen's jewels," he said.

"And they probably never will," his father said. "I'll bet some fence has them by now."

"*Fence?* What's that, Mr. Duncan?" Ruth Rose asked.

"*Fence* is a slang name for a person who buys stolen goods from robbers," Dink's father explained. "The crooks might have given the tiara and necklace to a fence. That person would sell them, then split the money with the robbers."

"We're going to find the jewels and get the reward!" Josh said. "It's fifteen thousand dollars!"

"Well, good luck," Mr. Duncan said. "Are you hungry?"

"Starved!" said Josh.

"Good. Take the rest of the pizza across the hall," Mr. Duncan said. He pointed to the pizza box on the coffee table. "I'm going to read for a while, then go back to my conference."

"What's the book, Dad?" Dink asked.

Mr. Duncan held it up. "Some stories by a writer named Edgar Allan Poe," he said. "I'm reading one called 'The Purloined Letter.' The story takes place in Paris, France."

"What's *purloined*?" Josh asked.

"*Purloined* means *stolen*," Mr. Duncan said. "In the story, the bad guy steals an important letter. He knows the police will come to his apartment to search. So the thief hides the letter in a clever place: in plain sight, next to some cards from visitors."

"The crook hid the letter right out in the open?" Josh said.

"That's right, Josh," Dink's father said. "He figured the police might search in obvious hiding places but not just look around the room. Pretty clever, eh?"

"Do the police find the letter?" Ruth Rose asked.

Dink's father smiled. "I'll let you read the story when I'm finished," he said.

The kids took the pizza, some napkins, and the newspaper to Dink and Josh's room. They flopped on the floor and started eating.

Dink pointed to the picture of Prince Harry on the front page of the newspaper. "Damon really does look a lot like Prince Harry," he said.

Josh and Ruth Rose studied the picture.

"Are you thinking what I'm thinking?" Ruth Rose asked Dink.

Dink nodded. "Yep," he said. "Damon and Harry are both tall, so if Damon was wearing Prince Harry's uniform, the queen might think Damon was her grandson!"

CHAPTER 7

Josh stared at Dink for a long minute. "Damon Fox stole the queen's jewels!" he whispered. "And he's right downstairs!"

Dink shrugged. "Maybe," he said.

Ruth Rose stared at the picture of Prince Harry. "I'm getting goose bumps!" she said.

Outside their window, lightning flashed. A loud clap of thunder shook the window. Raindrops made loud splatting sounds against the glass.

Ruth Rose looked at Dink and

Josh. "But if you were Damon and you planned to rob the queen's jewels, wouldn't you still wear a mask?" she asked. "It wouldn't matter if you looked like Prince Harry—you wouldn't want the queen to see your face."

"Right," Dink said. "And the other robber wouldn't want the queen to see *his* face, either. So I'll bet they both did wear masks."

"The queen told us there was something weird about the robbers' mouths," Josh said. "Maybe it was because their mouths were rubber!"

The kids were quiet for a minute, thinking.

"I wonder where the robbers got masks that looked like the queen's two grandsons," Ruth Rose said.

Once again, Dink tried to capture a thought that was buzzing around inside his head. It was the same thought he'd had earlier. *Why couldn't he remember?*

"We have to find out if Damon chews Summer Green gum," Josh said.

"And what color his car is," Ruth Rose added. "The queen saw a black car drive away!"

"But remember, there were two robbers," Dink said. "So maybe the second robber owned the car. Maybe the *second robber* was chewing Summer Green gum."

"Okay, so we also have to find out if Damon Fox has a tall friend," Ruth Rose said.

Dink helped himself to another slice of pizza. "I say we go back to the wax museum," he said.

"Why?" Josh asked. "We should spy on Damon!"

Dink took a bite, chewed, and swallowed. "Remember the story Dad was reading?" he asked. "The crook hid a letter where no one would think to look—in plain sight, with some other papers." Dink grinned at Josh and Ruth Rose. "So what if our crooks did the same thing?"

"You lost me," Josh said. "The crooks who stole the queen's jewels also stole a letter?"

"No, Dink means maybe the robbers hid the queen's jewels with some other jewels!" Ruth Rose said. "Right out in the open!"

"In a jewelry store!" Josh said.

"No, at the wax museum, right, Dink?" Ruth Rose asked.

Dink nodded. "Think about it," he said. "A million Scotland Yard detectives will be searching London for the queen's jewels. So if you were the crooks, maybe you'd hide them in the wax museum, where there's a lot of other jewelry. And Damon probably knows it's there."

"But how would Damon or the other robber get the stolen jewels into the museum?" Josh asked. "They couldn't just walk into the wardrobe room without Ian or Mandy or that seamstress lady stopping them."

"Maybe Damon could," Dink said. "He told us Ian is his cousin. And maybe he knows Mandy, too. Damon could have snuck into that room when they were busy. And the seamstress must leave the wardrobe room once in a while."

"Dink's right," Ruth Rose said. "It would take only a few seconds to put the real jewels on the shelf with the fake ones."

Dink nodded. "That's why I want to go back to the museum," he said, glancing out the window. "If this rain ever stops."

"I'll check the weather forecast," Ruth Rose said. She grabbed the remote and switched on the TV.

A woman with a bright smile told everyone the rain would continue until at least midnight.

Then a man took over. He said there was no news from Scotland Yard on the theft of the queen's tiara and necklace. The search for the stolen jewels and the robbers was ongoing.

He also said hospitals and clinics

had been alerted to watch for a tall man who came in with a dog bite.

"The queen reported that her dog Willow bit one of the robbers on his left hand," the newsman said. "Now back to our regular show."

Dink could feel his heartbeat speed up. "Guys, Damon has a round Band-Aid on the back of his left hand," he said.

"I didn't notice," Ruth Rose said. "But just because he has a Band-Aid doesn't mean he got bitten by the queen's dog."

"Maybe Damon got a paper cut," Josh suggested.

"How do you get a paper cut on the *back* of your hand?" Dink asked.

The storm soaked London all night. But by Tuesday morning, the sun was peeking from behind dark clouds. The weatherwoman promised a few more showers.

Dink's father left for his conference. The kids were still eating in the small dining room off the hotel lobby.

Ruth Rose had a clear view of Damon in the lobby.

"You were right about Damon," she whispered. "I can see the Band-Aid on the back of his left hand."

"I wonder if it's covering teeth marks," Dink said.

Josh sipped his apple juice. "If we find the jewels but not the robbers, do we still get the reward?" he asked.

"I think so," Dink said. "Ready to take off?"

The kids walked past Damon, who was on the telephone. They waved, and he waved back.

Dink felt a little guilty. Damon had been really nice to them, and here they

were, suspecting him of robbing the Queen of England! It wasn't Damon's fault that he just happened to look like the queen's grandson!

But what was under that round Band-Aid?

Outside the hotel, Ruth Rose snapped a picture of a cabdriver washing his cab. It was dark blue but looked black when he turned the hose on it. The cabdriver smiled and waved his wet sponge at the kids.

They hiked up Baker Street and crossed Marylebone Road. Up ahead, Dink could see a group of people waiting to get into Madame Tussauds. They were in front of door number two. A sign over the yellow door said GROUP ENTRANCE.

Just then, a dark green jeep passed the kids and pulled up in front of the wax museum.

They were close enough to see Mandy in the driver's seat. She and her passenger both stepped out. He was a tall man with sandy-colored hair. Mandy handed him the jeep keys.

Dink recognized him. He was the guy in the picture with Mandy that was pinned to her bulletin board.

"Hey, kids!" Mandy said when she saw them.

"We decided to come back," Ruth Rose said. "There's so much to see!"

"Cool," Mandy said. Then she turned to the man. "This is my big brother, Simon Clyde."

Simon and Mandy looked almost like twins. They were both tall, with blue eyes and wide smiles.

"Can I get a picture?" Ruth Rose asked. "I'm going to make a London scrapbook when I get home!"

Mandy and Simon leaned against

the jeep's rear bumper, and Ruth Rose snapped the picture.

"How about one of you four together?" Simon said. "Mandy, go stand with the kids." He reached for Ruth Rose's camera.

Ruth Rose handed the camera to Simon. "Just push that little silver button," she said.

Mandy and the kids bunched together.

"Closer," Simon said.

They squeezed closer. Dink was between Mandy and Ruth Rose. He could smell Mandy's spicy perfume.

Simon took the shot and handed the camera back to Ruth Rose.

"I'll pick you up at six," Simon said as he climbed into the jeep.

Mandy unlocked door number one of Madame Tussauds.

CHAPTER 8

As soon as they were inside, Mandy unlocked the other door, and the tourist group crowded in.

Dink looked around but didn't see Ian.

Suddenly Ruth Rose grabbed Dink and Josh and pulled them aside.

"What's going on?" Josh asked.

"That guy! He came in with the group," Ruth Rose whispered. "He's here again!"

"Who?" Dink asked.

"That artist guy we saw last time we

were here," she said. "Only today he looks different, and he doesn't have his sketch pad."

Dink and Josh peeked over Ruth Rose's shoulders. It was the same guy, all right. But he had shaved and was wearing a different hat.

"Why is he here twice in the same week?" Ruth Rose asked.

"And he isn't looking at the wax people," Dink said.

"And why is he wearing sunglasses inside?" Josh added.

The three kids kept their eyes on the man as he walked around the room.

"I'll bet he's one of the robbers!" Josh said.

"You said that about the gardener at Windsor Castle," Dink reminded him.

"He looks sneaky," Ruth Rose said. "Not like a regular tourist."

They watched the man until he disappeared through the black curtains.

"Guys, we came to check out the fake jewels in the wardrobe room," Dink reminded them.

The kids slowly made their way toward the wardrobe room. Dink kept an eye out for Ian but didn't see him. Mandy had taken the group to another part of the museum. Dink, Josh, and Ruth Rose were alone.

The door was partly open, and Dink peeked in. The room was empty. "Come on," he whispered.

The kids slipped into the wardrobe room, and Dink pulled the door almost closed.

Sofia's chair was empty. Her keys lay on her sewing table.

Dink glanced through the small window. He saw rain splashing on the glass. Traffic flashed by on Marylebone Road. Someone in tall boots hurried past the window.

Dink stepped over to the shelf that held all the fake diamond jewelry. "The queen said her tiara and necklace have her initials," he said. "So let's check this stuff."

They got busy.

There were only two tiaras on the shelf. Neither had any letters engraved on the fake silver.

Dink saw at least five fake diamond necklaces. The kids picked them up and checked for the letters *E.A.M.*

"No initials, guys," Josh whispered. "They're all fakes."

Dink felt disappointed. He'd convinced himself that a perfect place to hide the queen's stolen jewels was here, among this fake stuff.

"Hey, guys, check this out," Ruth Rose said. She was a few feet away, standing in front of a glass case. The case was labeled ROYAL FAMILY. Inside was a rack of outfits. Lined up on the floor were pairs of shoes that went with each outfit.

Dink and Josh walked over.

"See those two uniforms hanging next to each other?" Ruth Rose said. "We've seen them before."

She was pointing at a dark blue uniform jacket. On the next hanger was a red tunic with silver buttons.

"Those are the extras," Josh said. "Prince William and his brother Harry's statues are wearing them out in the other room."

"That's right," Ruth Rose said. "And the queen told us the robbers were wearing the same outfits. I wonder where the robbers *got* those outfits."

It took a minute before Dink realized what Ruth Rose was suggesting. He stared through the glass case. "Oh my gosh, you think the crooks wore *these*?" he said.

Ruth Rose nodded. "Where else would robbers get two uniforms just like the ones Prince William and Prince Harry wear?" she whispered.

She dashed over to Sofia's table and grabbed the key ring. She was back in a jiffy and inserted one of the keys into the glass case's lock.

"Ruth Rose, you can't just—" Josh started to say.

"Shhh," Ruth Rose said. "Keep your eye on the door!" She tried three more keys before the tiny lock clicked open. She slid the glass door aside and lifted the hanger that held the blue jacket. Under the jacket hung snow-white trousers. Pinned to the hanger was a pair of white cotton gloves. A small paper tag on one of the gloves said PRINCE WILLIAM.

Ruth Rose replaced the hanger and grabbed the one holding the red tunic. The white trousers were there, and a white belt with a shiny silver buckle.

But there were no white gloves. A tag that said PRINCE HARRY was pinned to the tunic.

"Where are Harry's gloves?" Ruth Rose asked. "The queen said both robbers were wearing white gloves."

"The dog bite," Dink said. "Maybe the glove got torn."

"And they wouldn't want to leave a torn glove here with these uniforms!" Ruth Rose said. "It might even have the robber's blood on it!"

"But, guys, how would the robbers *get* these uniforms?" Josh asked. "They couldn't just walk in here and take them."

Ruth Rose held up the keys. "Sofia could have let them in," she whispered.

"Sofia's in on it?" Josh asked. "Sofia and Damon are the robbers?"

Dink shook his head. "Sofia is too short to wear these uniforms," he said.

"But Ian is tall enough. Maybe he and Damon are the crooks. Two cousins pretending to be two brothers!"

"And Sofia could have helped them," Ruth Rose said. "She could have snuck out the uniforms, then hung them back where they belong after the robbery."

Ruth Rose picked up the shiny black shoes beneath the red tunic. She turned the shoes over and looked at the soles. "Check this out," she said.

The boys looked. The soles of both shoes had traces of mud on the leather. Stuck in the mud was a blade of grass. The other pair of shoes also had mud on the soles.

"Someone wore these shoes in a muddy place," Ruth Rose whispered.

Dink remembered the muddy grass outside the gate to Windsor Castle. He thought of the tire marks in that same area.

Suddenly Ruth Rose reached for the white belt that was hanging with the red tunic. She pulled the belt free and held the silver buckle close to her face.

"What're you doing?" Josh hissed.

"Whoever wore this belt last might

have left his fingerprints," Ruth Rose said, studying the buckle.

She rolled the belt and shoved it into her pack.

"I'll just take that, please," said a voice behind Ruth Rose.

CHAPTER 9

The three kids whirled around. A tall
man was standing inside the door, leaning on it.

It was the artist. Without the dark
glasses covering his eyes, he looked
angry.

Dink noticed that he was holding
something small and black.

"I'd like the belt," the man said. "And
handle it carefully, miss."

"Why do you want it?" Ruth Rose
asked. "It's only a belt."

The man opened the leather case

he'd been holding, revealing a gold badge. He stretched out the case so the kids could read the words stamped above the badge: INSPECTOR A. GRABBE, SCOTLAND YARD. "Now may I have the belt, please?"

"You're that detective from Scotland Yard!" Ruth Rose said. "Your name was in the paper."

The man nodded. "The belt?"

Ruth Rose pulled the rolled belt from her pack and handed it to Inspector Grabbe. "I wasn't going to steal it," Ruth Rose said. "We were just trying to find the robbers who stole the queen's jewels."

"Yes, me too," said the inspector. He peered closely at the buckle, then slipped the belt into a clear plastic bag. "And how are you doing?"

"We have some ideas," Dink said.

Finally, the man smiled. "I'd love to hear them," he said, moving into the room.

"So you're not really an artist?" Josh asked.

Inspector Grabbe shook his head. "That was just my cover," he said, grinning. "I've been keeping an eye on one of the museum employees. When I saw you three sneak in here, I decided to follow you. Now if you'd like to tell me what you know, you can go back to Welcome House."

"You know where we're staying?" Dink asked.

The inspector nodded. "I've been watching one of the employees there, too."

"Is it Damon?" Ruth Rose asked. "His cousin Ian works here. Were you watching them both?"

The man didn't answer. "What brought you kids to the wardrobe room today?" he asked instead.

"My father told us about a crook in a story who hid a letter right out in the open," Dink said. He went on to explain why he thought the missing diamonds might also be hidden in the open.

"Not a bad idea," Inspector Grabbe said.

"We talked to the queen yesterday,"

Josh said. "She told us the real diamonds, the ones the crooks stole from her, had her initials on them—*E.A.M.* So we came in here to check all the jewelry." Josh pointed to the jewelry on the shelf. "If we find the initials, that means the diamonds are real, not fake."

"You spoke to the queen?" the detective said.

Ruth Rose explained how they went to Windsor Castle to look for clues.

"Did you find any?"

"We think we saw where the getaway car was parked," Dink said. He reached into his pocket. "And we found this."

He handed the foil wrapper to the detective. "One of the robbers could have dropped it," Dink said.

The detective read the name. "Summer Green? Never heard of it." He smelled the inside of the gum wrapper. "Nice. Kind of spicy."

Dink leaned back and blinked. Where had he just smelled something else that was spicy?

"That's not all," Ruth Rose said. "We think the robbers borrowed the uniforms they were wearing from that glass case. There's grass and mud on the shoes!"

The inspector nodded. "I'll have my team check those uniforms and the belt buckle. But even if fingerprints show up, whose prints are they?"

"It could be Damon Fox," Josh said. "He has a bandage on his hand, and the queen said her dog bit one of the guys!"

"Damon Fox has an alibi," Inspector Grabbe said. "He was visiting his mother Saturday when the robbery took place. And that bandage is a patch his doctor gave him to help him quit smoking. No dog bit his hand."

"Oh my gosh," Dink said suddenly.

"*Oh my gosh* what?" Josh said.

"Mandy's perfume," Dink muttered. "It's spicy."

"What's that?" the detective asked.

"Mandy's brother was taking our picture outside," Dink said. "I stood next to Mandy and I smelled her perfume. But now I don't think it was perfume. It was her gum! It has the same spicy smell as the gum wrapper!"

Josh and Ruth Rose stared at Dink.

Dink felt his hands getting sweaty. "Maybe Mandy dropped that gum wrapper where the getaway car was parked," he said. "Maybe she's one of the robbers!"

"It would be easy for her to get those uniforms," Ruth Rose said.

"And she's tall enough to wear one of them!" Josh said.

"But who wore the other one?" Dink asked.

No one had an answer. Dink heard

thunder and glanced through the window. It had started to rain harder, turning the street shiny. He watched cars streak by, throwing off water. The wet cars looked black.

"What about Simon?" Dink asked. "He's tall, too."

"Who's Simon?" Inspector Grabbe asked.

Ruth Rose pulled her camera out of her pack. She found the picture she'd snapped of Mandy and Simon leaning against his jeep. "Simon is Mandy's brother," she said. She handed over the camera. "That's him right there."

The detective stared at the picture, then passed the camera back to Ruth Rose. He sighed. "We have no proof. Mandy *may* have access to those uniforms," he said. "And she *may* chew Summer Green gum. I'll bet millions of people chew it, too. But that's not enough evidence to arrest her. Matter of fact, it's not evidence at all."

"But what if you find *her* fingerprints on the belt buckle?" Ruth Rose asked.

Inspector Grabbe shrugged. "Mandy works here. She could easily explain why her fingerprints are on that belt," he said. "Her prints there wouldn't prove she wore the uniform to commit a robbery."

Suddenly Josh grabbed the camera. He examined the picture of Mandy and Simon. "What's that behind their legs on the car?" he asked. "On the bumper!"

Ruth Rose and Dink studied the picture with Josh.

"It looks like a bumper sticker," Dink said. "You can see part of the words. The rest is muddy."

"I can make out *DAME* and *US-SAUD*," Ruth Rose said. "Oh, I know. It says *MADAME TUSSAUDS*. The museum sells bumper stickers. Mandy must have put one on the car."

"But look at it now!" Josh said. He ran over to the sink and held the camera in front of the mirror.

Now the letters read *DUASSU* and *EMAD*.

"Oh my gosh!" Dink said again. "Those are the letters the queen saw on the getaway car!"

"Let me see that!" Inspector Grabbe took the camera from Josh's hand. "You kids are right!" he said. "She told me about the letters she saw, but they didn't make sense."

He smiled at the kids. "Now they *do* make sense!" he said. "The queen was seeing a Madame Tussauds bumper sticker. But since she was seeing it in her car's rearview mirror, she read the letters backward!"

CHAPTER 10

"So the crooks *are* Mandy and Simon!" Ruth Rose said. "And Simon's jeep is the getaway car that the queen saw!"

"The queen saw a black car, though," Josh said. "Simon's jeep is green."

"But it was raining," Dink said. He pointed out the window. "Dark cars look black when they get wet!"

Inspector Grabbe smiled. "How'd you kids get so smart?" he asked.

Josh tapped his head. "Mighty Josh brains," he said.

Everyone laughed.

"I just thought of something else," Ruth Rose said. "Simon's fingerprints are on my camera. So if they match the ones you find on the buckle, that means *he* wore the belt, right?"

Inspector Grabbe nodded and slipped the camera into another clear bag. "I'll give it back later," he told Ruth Rose.

Just then, the thought that Dink had been chasing popped into his head. "Did the queen say anything to you about the robbers wearing rubber masks?" he asked the inspector.

"Nope. She just said they looked like her two grandsons," he said. "Why?"

"Because *someone* told us the robbers were wearing lifelike rubber masks," Dink said. "We thought we read it in the paper, but now I remember who told us. It was Mandy. But how would she know about the masks if no one else did?"

"Of course. Only the thieves would know about the masks," the inspector said. "The queen never mentioned them, so I didn't know. And the newspapers didn't know, either. If Mandy said the crooks wore masks, she must have known firsthand!"

"And she knows how to make masks!" Josh said. "She said so! So can you arrest Mandy and Simon? Do we get the reward?"

The inspector smiled. "What would you do with ten thousand pounds?" he asked.

"Buy a helicopter!" Josh said. "I'd fly all around the world with my sketch pad. I'd be a flying artist!"

"I'm afraid I can't arrest them yet," Inspector Grabbe said. "If I did, they could clam up about the stolen jewelry. We'd never find it! And without the queen's jewelry, we can't prove those two were the crooks."

"But what if we *could* find the jewelry?" Dink asked. "And what if Mandy's fingerprints were on it?"

"Then we'd have a slam dunk," Inspector Grabbe said. He gave Dink a look. "Do you know something?"

Dink nodded. "In that story my dad told us about, 'The Purloined Letter,' the crook hid the letter right where no one would look, out in the open, with some other papers. So we looked for the queen's jewels on the shelf with a bunch of fake jewelry. Only they weren't there."

The inspector nodded. "Go on."

Dink lowered his voice. "But we didn't look in the right place," he said.

"So what is the right place?" Inspector Grabbe asked.

"I think the queen's jewelry is on her wax figure," Dink said. "Right out in plain sight."

"Here, in the wax museum?" Inspector Grabbe asked. "On the queen?"

"Mandy told us the tiara and necklace on the queen's wax figure were fake!" Josh said.

"Sure she did," Dink said. "And they *were* fake before the robbery. But after the robbery, I think Mandy took the fake stuff off the queen's wax figure and put the real jewels on her! It's a perfect hiding place!"

"You know that red rope they have around the figures of the Royal Family?" Ruth Rose asked. "No other statue has a rope. Mandy said it was to keep people from touching the queen, but I'll bet it's so people can't get a close look at the jewels she's wearing!"

"If you're right, this is amazing!" Inspector Grabbe said. "Police and detectives are combing every corner of London for the queen's jewels. They're questioning every known fence. But the jewels end up where no one would dream of looking—on the wax queen!"

"Let's go check it out!" Josh said.

"Not so fast," the Scotland Yard inspector said. He pulled a cell phone out of his pocket. "I need backup."

"We can be your backup!" Josh said.

Inspector Grabbe smiled. "Tempting," he said. "You kids *are* smart, but I need *big* and smart." He tapped a number into his cell phone and began talking.

◆ ◆ ◆

Twenty minutes later, two detectives, a man and a woman, arrived outside the wax museum. They were wearing regular clothes so they wouldn't stand out.

Inspector Grabbe gave the backup team orders, then sent them inside. Once they were in place, he led the kids back into the museum.

They walked up to the figure of the Queen of England. "I hope we're right," Inspector Grabbe muttered. "Otherwise, this could get embarrassing!"

He unclipped the velvet rope from one of its poles. "Hold this," he said to Dink, handing him the end of the rope.

The inspector walked around the pole and behind the queen. Gently, he unclasped her necklace and held it close to his eyes. He smiled. "Bingo," he said.

"Excuse me, what are you doing?" demanded an angry voice.

It was Mandy. She was standing with

a small group of tourists. Her face was red, and Dink thought her eyes looked scared.

Inspector Grabbe turned toward Mandy, holding the necklace. "Tell me, Ms. Clyde. Does the museum's fake jewelry have initials on the metal? The letters *E.A.M.*, to be exact?"

Mandy didn't answer. Her mouth opened, but no words came out.

"Ms. Clyde, if I show this necklace to the queen, will she think it's fake?" Inspector Grabbe asked. "Or will she recognize it as the one you and Simon stole from her?"

Mandy's face went from red to white.

"Also, Ms. Clyde," the inspector went on, dangling the necklace in front of Mandy, "when I check this necklace and tiara for fingerprints, whose will I find, yours or your brother's?"

Suddenly Mandy snatched the neck-

lace out of Inspector Grabbe's fingers. She raced past the queen's figure, grabbing the tiara with her other hand.

Mandy bolted for the exit, knocking Dink to the floor as she raced past him.

As Dink fell, he threw his hands out in front of him. He was still holding one end of the velvet rope. The rope stretched tight, dragging a pole toward Dink.

Mandy tried to leap over the pole,

but her feet became tangled in the rope. She stumbled and fell on top of Dink. When she tried to stand, Dink yanked on the rope. Mandy was tied like a calf at a rodeo.

The two backup detectives ran over. They lifted Mandy to her feet and took the jewelry out of her hands. Dink noticed Band-Aids on two fingers on her left hand. He was positive they were covering the bite marks from the queen's dog Willow.

"Nice grab!" Inspector Grabbe told Dink.

Dink tapped the side of his head. "Easy peasy," he said.

CHAPTER 11

At noon the next day, the kids and Dink's father hopped out of a cab in front of Buckingham Palace. The boys wore their best shirts and pants. Ruth Rose wore red—all red.

A row of guards stood in front of the palace entrance. They wore tall, furry hats, red jackets, and black pants. One of the guards marched toward the kids.

"He's going to put you in a dungeon," Dink whispered to Josh.

The guard stopped in front of Ruth Rose. "The queen is waiting," he said.

"Will you follow me, please?"

Just then, a bright yellow helicopter came thudding out of the sky over the palace. It slowed, then disappeared behind the building.

"That's what I'm going to buy with my part of the reward money," Josh said.

"Good luck," Dink said. "You couldn't even buy one of the wheels with one-third of fifteen thousand dollars."

Dink, Josh, Ruth Rose, and Dink's father followed the guard. He was tall and took long strides, so they had to run to keep up. The guard went around a corner and stopped at a small private door. He knocked, and the door opened. Another guard stood inside.

The first guard left, and the kids followed the second one down a long corridor.

Dink felt like giggling. He couldn't believe they were really in Buckingham

Palace, about to meet the Queen of England! Of course, they had already met her, but this felt different.

The guard stopped in front of a door where a third guard stood. The second guard bowed to the kids and headed back the way they had come. The third guard knocked on the door, waited three seconds, then opened it. "Visitors, mum," the guard said.

The Queen of England was sitting near a fireplace. A cheery fire made the room cozy. Three brown-and-white dogs lay at the queen's feet. The dogs were no longer wet and muddy. They were all watching as the kids and Dink's father stepped into the room.

The queen stood up. "Thank you for coming," she said. She reached out her hand.

They all shook hands.

"I thank you—my whole family

thanks you—for finding my jewels," the queen said. "What clever children!"

The queen looked much better not wearing a raincoat and muddy boots.

Dink's father smiled. "We raise smart kids in Connecticut," he said.

"Please sit and tell me all about it," the queen said. They moved to another part of the room. "I hope you're hungry."

The three kids gasped. A table was heaped with trays of food. One held small cakes with colored frosting. Another tray was full of cookies and some whipped-creamy things they'd never seen before. There were tiny sandwiches made with bread with the crusts cut off. A bowl of fruit gleamed under the lights.

Next to the food stood a silver teapot and a pitcher of lemonade. There were cloth napkins and silver spoons and forks. The cups and saucers had

gold edges. Everything was arranged on a snow-white tablecloth.

The queen sat first, then the others. "Help yourselves, please," she said.

The queen poured tea while the kids and Dink's father filled their plates.

When everyone had their food, the kids told the queen about the clues: the bumper sticker, the tire marks in the mud, the gum wrapper, the spicy smell

that Dink had thought was Mandy's perfume.

"We were really sure after we saw the mud on the black shoes in the wardrobe room," Ruth Rose added.

"And the robbers *were* wearing rubber masks," Dink said. "When I finally remembered that Mandy told us that, I wondered how she would know. Then it hit me: she'd know if she made the masks herself! She and her brother wore them when they robbed you."

The queen nodded. "Very clever," she said. "My grandsons remembered talking to Mandy about my birthday surprise the day they went in to have their pictures taken," she said. "That girl and her brother must have begun planning the robbery that very day."

"What will happen to Mandy and Simon?" Josh asked. "Will you lock them up in a dungeon?"

The queen smiled. "The Windsor Castle dungeon hasn't held prisoners in many years," she said. "But those two aren't British citizens. They'll be sent back to the United States, where I have been assured they will visit one of your fine prisons."

The queen pushed a small button on the arm of her chair. A few seconds later, a man in a gray suit came in, carrying an envelope. He bowed, handed it to the queen, then disappeared.

The queen handed the envelope to Josh. "Here is your reward," she said. "For your service to the Crown!"

Dink's father plucked the envelope from Josh's fingers.

"Thank you," he said. "This will go into a college fund for these three young detectives."

The queen smiled. "One more thing," she said. She looked at Josh. "You remind me of my grandson Harry when he was your age. He loved helicopters, and I hear that you do as well. Is that true, Joshua?"

Josh grinned. "How did you know?"

The queen tapped her head. "I have spies," she said. Then she pushed the button again. The door behind her opened. Prince William and Prince Harry walked into the room. They were

wearing the same uniforms the kids had seen at the museum.

The queen beamed at her handsome grandsons. "Hello, boys," she said. "Did you bring it?"

"It's parked out back, Granny," Prince William said.

Prince Harry grinned at Josh. "I hear you've never been in a helicopter," he said.

"Yes, sir," Josh managed to say. "I mean, no, sir!"

"Well, that will change today," Prince William said. "Are you kids ready to go for a chopper ride over London?"

Josh jumped up out of his chair. "Really?" he said. "You're not teasing?"

"The Royal Family never teases!" Prince Harry said. "Let's go!"

"Can I take a cookie with me?" Josh asked.

"Yes," Prince William said.

"Can I sit next to the pilot?" Josh asked.

"Yes," Prince Harry said.

"Can I fly the chopper?" Josh asked.

"NO!" everyone yelled.

A to Z Mysteries

Dear Readers,

I receive a lot of questions from kids who read my books, and I try to answer them all. One thing many kids want to know is where I get the ideas for my books. My ideas come from many places: from my reading, from traveling, from talking to people, and from keeping aware of the world around me.

In the past few years, there has been a lot of news about the Royal Family in London. When I learned that the Queen of England likes to drive her own car, I was intrigued. Yes, she has bodyguards for protection and she has a chauffeur to drive her places. But sometimes she likes to be alone in her car, and that is what gave me the idea for *The Castle Crime.* I asked myself, what if the queen got robbed while she was driving her car without her bodyguards?

As for most of my books, I had to do some research. I needed to know more about the queen and the Royal Family. I also had to learn about Buckingham Palace, where the queen lives most of the time, and Windsor Castle, where she sometimes spends holidays and weekends.

I do my research by reading books on a subject, by talking to experts, and often by going to the place I'm researching. I visited London a couple of years before I decided to set this book there. For information about the Madame Tussauds wax museum, I toured the one in New York City.

I hope you enjoy reading *The Castle Crime* as much as I enjoyed researching, planning, and writing it.

Happy reading!

Sincerely,

Ron Roy

Did you find the secret message hidden in this book?

If you *don't* want to know the answer, *don't* look at the bottom of this page!

Answer:
IS JACK THE RIPPER THE NEXT CASE?

Illustration © 2013 by John Steven Gurney

Calendar Mysteries

Help Bradley, Brian, Lucy, and Nate . . .

. . . solve a mystery a month!